THE JUPITER STONE

PAUL OWEN LEWIS

TRICYCLE PRESS
Berkeley | Toronto

TRICYCLE PRESS
a little division of Ten Speed Press
P.O. Box 7123
Berkeley, California 94707
www.tenspeed.com

Book design by Betsy Stromberg
Typeset in Papyrus ICG

Library of Congress Cataloging-in-Publication Data

Lewis, Paul Owen.
  The Jupiter stone / Paul Owen Lewis.
    p. cm.
Summary: When a young boy finds a rock that had floated through space
and landed on Earth millions of years earlier, he writes a letter to
NASA asking them to return it to the heavens.
  ISBN 1-58246-107-4
  [1. Rocks—Fiction.] I. Title.
  PZ7.L58765 Ju 2003
  [E]—dc21

                        2002155291

First Tricycle Press Printing, 2003
1 2 3 4 5 6 — 07 06 05 04 03

To Jennifer

A small striped stone
tumbled in the vastness
of space...

·until it crossed
the path
of one planet
among many...

and joined countless
other stones there.

Millions of years passed...

and passed...

and passed...

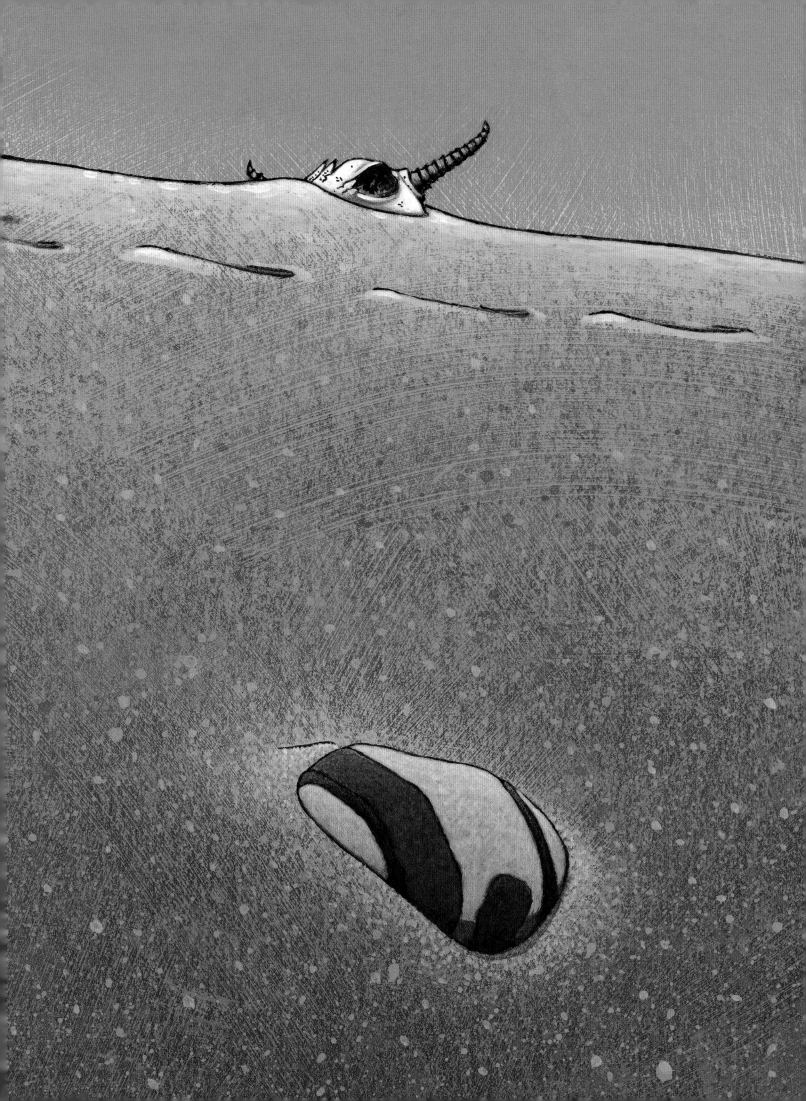

until one day,
a child found it.

"Look, Mom, this one looks like
the planet Jupiter," he said.

"Wow. It's beautiful. Where do you think it came from?" she asked.

Inspired by the answer
he found, the boy
wrote a letter...

and the stone was launched
into orbit.

It was sent away...

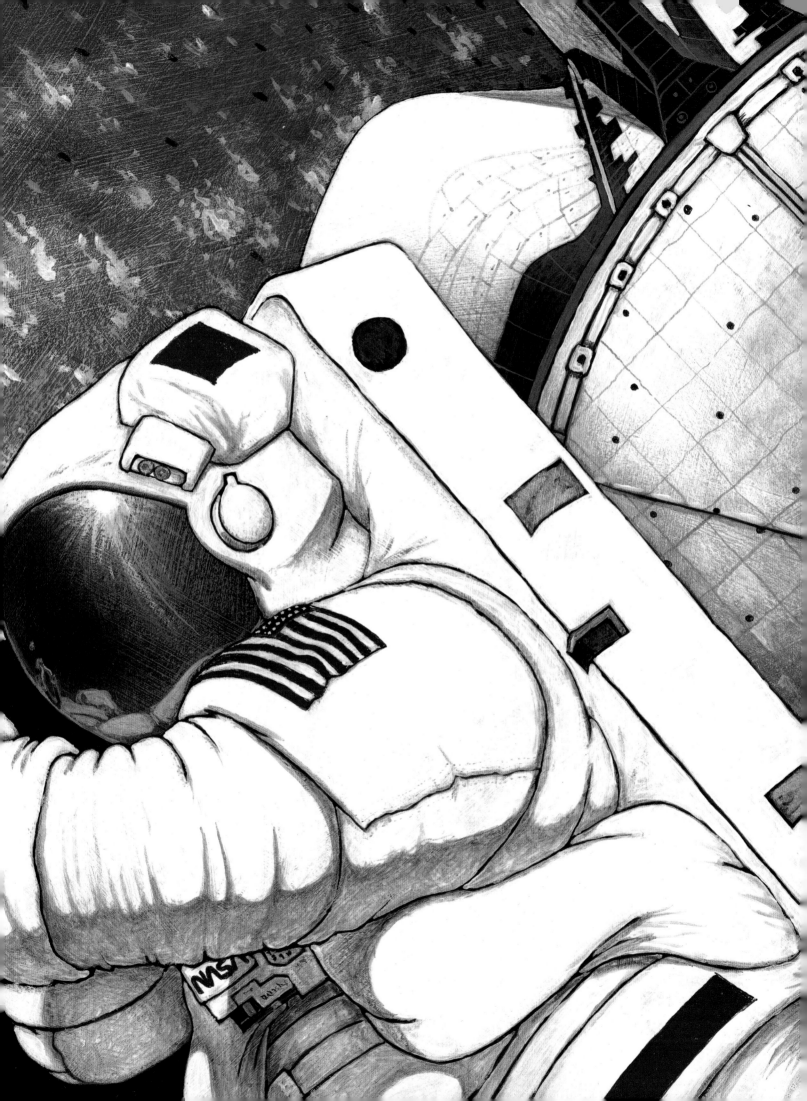

to tumble again in the vastness of space.

Until
one day...

a child
found it.

To see a world in a grain of sand

And heaven in a wild flower,

Hold infinity in the palm of your hand

And eternity in an hour.

-WILLIAM BLAKE